As Alice sits under a tree one lazy summer afternoon, little does she know what adventures lie in store for her...

It all begins when a White Rabbit appears from nowhere, peering at his pocket watch and muttering to himself. He leads Alice down a deep rabbit hole, where she meets many strange and wonderful characters.

British Library Cataloguing in Publication Data
Walt Disney's Alice in Wonderland.—(Disney stories)
 I. Series
 823´.914[J]   PZ7
  ISBN 0-7214-1059-6

First edition

Published by Ladybird Books Ltd Loughborough Leicestershire UK

Printed in England (7)

DISNEP

ALICE in WONDERLAND

Ladybird Books

One hot summer's day, a little girl named Alice sat up in a tree. She was supposed to be listening to her grown-up sister read out an important history lesson.

But it wasn't very interesting, for it had no pictures in it. Alice began to feel sleepy.

She climbed down from the tree and rested beneath it. Just as she closed her eyes, a white rabbit came scuttling by.

Alice sat up in surprise. The White Rabbit was wearing a bright red jacket!

The White Rabbit looked at a pocket
watch as he ran.

"I'm late!" Alice heard him say.
"Oh dear, oh dear, oh dear! I'm late!"

"Wait for me!" called Alice.

But the White Rabbit replied, "I've no
time! I'm late, I'm late, I'm late!"

Alice was curious, and she watched as
he disappeared into a hole at the foot of
a tree.

Alice decided to follow him. At first she had to crawl along but suddenly she found herself falling down into the darkness.

Then she was floating! Soon there was enough light to see furniture of all kinds floating past her head.

When at last she landed, Alice discovered that she was in an enormous room. On the ground was a little door with a big brass doorknob. She knelt on the floor and tried to peep through the keyhole.

"Eek!" cried a tiny voice, and Alice realised that the doorknob had spoken. "What *are* you doing?"

"Following the White Rabbit," answered Alice. "Please let me through!"

"You're too big for the door," replied the doorknob. "You must drink the contents of that bottle."

Alice looked round and noticed a small table. On it stood a bottle with a label which read *drink me*.

So Alice uncorked the bottle and drank some of the mixture inside it.

All at once she began to shrink, and soon she was small enough to get through the little door.

Alice was now standing in a garden, and in the distance she could see the White Rabbit. She started to run after him but, suddenly, her way was blocked by twin boys, each shaped like an Easter egg.

"I'm Tweedle Dum!" said one.

"I'm Tweedle Dee!" said the other.

"Who are *you*?" they said together. "And what do you want?"

Alice told them her name, and explained that she was curious to know about the White Rabbit. She could see that he was darting in and out of some bushes on the other side of the garden.

"Where is he?" she cried impatiently.

"Here, there, and everywhere!" sniggered the twins. And then they skipped away.

Alice ran off the other way, and came to a funny little house with a circular front door.

Suddenly, an upstairs window popped open and there was the White Rabbit! He was now dressed as a page in a frilly ruff.

"I'm seven minutes and seventy seconds late!" he cried unhappily. "And I've lost my gloves. Come and help me to find them!"

So Alice went into the house. She searched everywhere. She didn't find any gloves, but she did find a box of sweets.

Without stopping to think, she ate one.
And Alice started to grow, and grow,
and GROW!

Soon she grew too big for the house.
"Oh, my paws and whiskers!" cried the
White Rabbit. "Here's a monster in my
house! Oh dear, oh dear, oh dear!"

And away he ran.

But Alice fished about outside with her hand till she found a carrot growing in the garden. She nibbled it, and – sure enough! – she began to shrink again.

She ran out into the woods to find the White Rabbit again. Soon she had to stop for a rest.

"And who might you be?" asked a sleepy voice.

There, stretched out along a leaf, was a caterpillar.

"I'm Alice," she replied. "And I wish I was a little taller so that I could run faster."

"I can help you to grow if you like," said the Caterpillar, trying to stop yawning. "One side will make you grow taller, the other side will make you grow shorter."

"One side of what?" asked Alice, anxiously.

"The mushroom you're sitting on!" gasped the Caterpillar. Then, suddenly, he turned into a butterfly and flitted away.

Alice ate a piece of mushroom and soon
reached her normal height. She put
some bits of mushroom into her pocket
in case she ever needed them again.

As she walked on into the woods, she noticed an odd-looking cat with purple stripes sitting in a tree, watching her. It grinned. Then, to Alice's astonishment, it faded away – all except the grin, which stayed where it was.

"Goodness!" said Alice. "I do believe I've met the Cheshire Cat!"

The Cheshire Cat reappeared and told
Alice that she might find the White
Rabbit at the Mad Hatter's house, or
else at the March Hare's. So Alice
walked on, and came to a tea table set
with a great many places.

The Mad Hatter and the March Hare
were sitting there, singing. Alice sat
down. "Is this a birthday party?"
she asked.

"Certainly not!" replied the Mad
Hatter. "It's an un-birthday party. By
celebrating our un-birthdays, we can
have a party every day of the year."

The March Hare asked Alice where she had come from.

"Well," answered Alice, "I was sitting with Dinah, my cat – "

"Cat?" said a squeaky voice. "Did someone say *cat*?" –

A dormouse poked his head out of a teapot, in which he had been having a nap. Then he jumped out and ran about the table in panic.

"Catch him!" cried the Mad Hatter. "We must put some jam on his nose!"

Alice thought to herself, "I'm tired of all this. I'm going home."

As Alice left the tea table, the Cheshire Cat's grin suddenly appeared in a tree. "Why not go and look for the Queen?" he said.

Alice was thrilled at the idea, so she walked on until she came to a big garden full of white roses. To her amazement, a lot of playing cards, dressed as gardeners, were painting all the roses red!

They explained to Alice that the Queen of Hearts had ordered red roses, so they were painting the white ones, hoping that she wouldn't notice.

Just then the White Rabbit appeared
with a trumpet, and Alice realised that
he must be the Queen's herald. "The
Queen is coming!" he shouted.

The Queen of Hearts immediately saw
what the gardeners had been up to.

"Off with their heads!" she snapped.
Then she turned on Alice, and said,
"Who are you?"

Alice trembled and replied, "I'm a little
girl, and I've lost my way."

"All the ways round here belong to
me!" said the Queen. "Off with her
head!"

Then the Queen changed her mind and asked Alice to have a game of croquet. "Everyone to their places!" she shouted.

But no sooner had the game started than everyone began shouting and arguing. To add to the confusion, the Cheshire Cat kept appearing and disappearing in a most annoying manner. The Queen could stand it no longer. "Off with its head!" she screamed.

But the Cheshire Cat's head faded away, leaving behind only its grin.

The Queen was so angry that she ordered the White Rabbit to take Alice to the courthouse for trial.

"You are charged with the crime of cheating at croquet," he announced, "and also with tiring the Queen and making her lose her patience."

"Well said!" shouted the Queen. "Off with her head!"

"Shouldn't we hear the evidence first?" asked the King.

"If we must!" the Queen snapped at him. "Call the witnesses."

The first witness was the March Hare.
He cleared his throat and said, "I have
nothing to say."

Then came the Dormouse, and finally
the Mad Hatter marched to the front.
He wished the Queen a happy
un-birthday, offered his best wishes,
and went away.

At that moment the Cheshire Cat
appeared again. "Look!" cried Alice.
"The Cheshire Cat!"

Immediately the Dormouse jumped out
of his teapot. He ran up and down
squeaking and everyone ran after him.

Alice knew that she must escape. Then she remembered the mushroom in her pocket! She ate a piece and soon she towered above the court.

Turning to the Queen, Alice cried, "You don't frighten me; you're only an ugly, wicked, old Queen!"

Alice then swallowed another piece of
mushroom to make herself smaller,
hoping that no one would notice her as
she ran away.

But they did notice her! Through the
royal maze they chased her, but Alice
ran and ran.

At last she found herself standing once more in front of the little door with the brass doorknob.

Alice cried, "Please let me through! Let me through…"

Then she heard a kind voice saying, "Wake up, Alice! Tell me what you learned today in history." It was her big, grown-up sister smiling down at her!

Alice blinked and rubbed her eyes.
There was Dinah, curled up in her lap!

"I've had such an exciting time!" said
Alice. "There was a White Rabbit, and
I was curious, so I followed him, and...
and... and..." Alice's adventures
in Wonderland were over!